John Maxwell

True Reform

Character a qualification for the Franchise

John Maxwell

True Reform

Character a qualification for the Franchise

ISBN/EAN: 9783337295127

Printed in Europe, USA, Canada, Australia, Japan

Cover: Foto ©Andreas Hilbeck / pixelio.de

More available books at **www.hansebooks.com**

TRUE REFORM:

OR

CHARACTER A QUALIFICATION FOR THE FRANCHISE.

BY

SIR JOHN MAXWELL, BARONET.

Τεθνάμεναι γὰρ καλὸν ἐπὶ προμάχοισι πεσόντα
Ἀνδρ' ἀγαθὸν, περὶ ᾗ πατρίδι μαρνάμενον.
Τὴν δ' αὐτοῦ προλιπόντα πόλιν καὶ πίονας ἀγροὺς
Πτωχεύειν, πάντων, ἐστ' ἀνιηρότατον.

Among the foremost for our homes to die,
   In this there is a true nobility;
But sad the lot of him who leaves his land,
   To live an outcast on some foreign strand:
Compelled of haughty strangers bread to crave,
   And die unpitied like an abject slave;
Or see his children and his youthful wife,
   End in dire want their miserable life!—TYRTÆUS.

EDINBURGH: THOMAS CONSTABLE AND CO.
HAMILTON, ADAMS, AND CO., LONDON.
MDCCCLX.

EDINBURGH : T. CONSTABLE,
PRINTER TO THE QUEEN, AND TO THE UNIVERSITY.

PREFACE.

In reconstructing the laws which regulate the Elective Franchise, there are two objects which ought never to be lost sight of :—The first is, that these laws should secure a full and fair representation of all the interests of the country in Parliament ; and the second is, that they should, as far as possible, subserve the education of the people ; that is to say, foster the development of their character both morally and intellectually, so that they may be all duly protected, especially those that most need protection, as being least able to protect themselves.

It is my object in the following pages to show cases in which the existing laws might be modified by a due consideration of these objects ; and to try to suggest what that modification ought to be—not attempting to observe any formal order, but taking the leading features of the system as they present themselves.

INTRODUCTORY.

LABOUR is the source of all wealth. By the hand of the labouring man the earth is compelled to yield her stores, and without that hand the earth would remain unproductive. The workman, therefore, according to Burke, is the first creditor of the State, because without the fruit of his labour there could not be a State—there could not exist any institutions, social or political.* And yet because it rarely happens that, in this country, agricultural labourers live in houses of £10 rent, they are, by the present law, practically excluded from all share in the elective franchise. A large proportion of the whole amount of labour, both in towns and in the country, is performed by young unmarried men, who generally lodge in the houses of others ; and thus, although they may be more earnest, more energetic and more unselfish than many elder men, they also are excluded from the franchise by the law which confines that privilege to those who hold houses of £10 rent.

Very few soldiers or sailors have houses of the required rent ; and thus, though they have assisted at

* See Appendix, p. 48,—*Labour Capital.*

the hazard of their lives to gain security and scope
for every employment of capital through the country,
and though they may have received the thanks of
their sovereign and their country for their energy
and self-sacrificing courage, they yet have no voice
in the election of members of Parliamen t.

Yet the British Government can never be less indebted to the soldier and sailor who defend it—to
the workmen who, on sterile soils and stormy seas,
provide its bread, its fish, its fuel and metallic ores ; to
those who, living in villages or in small towns, conduct
machinery and carry on the works and manufactures
which enrich the capitalist—than to those who sell
provisions and fuel and manufactured goods of all
kinds, in well-sheltered shops and market-places,
or who gain their franchise by profits on the sale of
spirits ; or worse, by letting apartments to men and
women of bad character.

Men being too often sensual or money-making, we
need to acknowledge every indication of goodness and
of intelligence as a qualification for a trust which
should not be exercised for personal appetites but for
the public good, and cannot be justly or wisely confined to any specific rental as the guarantee for
purity of election.

The wish to be acknowledged by the Constitution
as a member of the national family is not only

natural but laudable. Habits of self-restraint and self-control may be strengthened, and fortitude and enterprise lighted up, by the prospect of power and respect reflected from a share in the franchise ; and perseverance in spite of obstacles, whether to secure independence or to gain an improved social position, may originate from this reasonable ambition.

Such aspirations and habits of life, like sentiments of integrity and truth, are not peculiar to any rank or station, and certainly ought to be both encouraged and cultivated in the working classes, as far as possible, by the laws and institutions of the country. These are never what they ought to be unless they tend to the moral improvement and mental and physical development of the people.

Working men must toil, but it does not follow that they will be frugal and temperate ; yet without self-restraint they cannot continue independent. They and their wives and families must come under obligations to, and end in being the debtors of, others, whose tools they may ultimately become, and so disqualify themselves for a right exercise of the franchise. Thus it is necessary, for the benefit of all classes, to restrict the right of voting in the case of such improvident day-labourers and operatives as are most exposed to the temptation of being induced to vote, as well as to work, on such terms as their employers may offer. The State is bound in duty to adopt every method by which the condition and dignity of the working classes may be elevated and maintained, and to bear in mind that any test of elective qualification by which these are disregarded and character neglected, inflicts a blow on the security and wellbeing of the whole community. It is of supreme importance that the institutions of their country should fortify and cherish men's inducements to be industrious, frugal, and self-denying; for these are the truest sources and means of independence to the workman, and of wealth and of power to the Empire.

For, unless the State treats the labouring energy of the industrious as part of the wealth of the country, and seeks, by the laws which are passed in Parliament, to foster and encourage it, the danger is, in these days of invention, that machinery will supplant men, and that the energetic and adventurous labourer will emigrate, and the feeble, timid, and idle alone remain. It is therefore wise and equitable that those who create capital, as well as those who accumulate it, should be considered in the financial policy of the State, and should not be unrepresented in the House of Commons.

If that security, which is indispensable to the monied man to induce him to keep his wealth in Britain, is provided by the laws, it seems fair that industry, which is the capital of the labourer, should also be guarded, and that those who have to make their fortune should be made the object of like careful preservation from unequal or excessive taxation with those whose fortunes are already secured. All fortunes are made out of the earnings of the skilful, the laborious, the prudent, or the daring, and are ultimately secured by the arms of warriors who, by sea and land, secure the power and independence of the country.

There is a saying, that the State has only to increase the capital of the rich, and to protect it, to insure the benefit of the working classes. If working classes mean labourers in all parts of the world, this is, to a certain extent, true ; but if the term be confined to native workmen, it is unfounded. Capital of money goes where it is most profitable and is most safely transferred. Capital of labour is transferred even from one trade to another, with difficulty and loss, it being always annoying and sometimes impossible, to find a new occupation when an existing one ceases to be remunerative. When land is no longer tilled, but laid down into pasture, when handwork is supplanted by mechanical power, manual labour must for a time be in excess, and necessarily falls in value. And further, as it is sometimes the misfortune of even the very best workmen, from commercial and manufacturing embarrassments, from war, and from the vicissitudes of climate, to be deprived of work, every possible mode of sustaining their confidence, cultivating their prudent habits, and making them sure of their recompense, ought to be resorted to by the State, and talents and industry be repre-

sented in conjunction with wealth and professional
knowledge and science.

In another view, also, the prosperity of what
may be called Labour Capital, is of the utmost importance to the safety of the State. Workmen unemployed are not only useless, but costly and danger-
ous! The hardened steal, the timid cheat; the rest,
in sorrow, apply to the parish for relief, but frequently not before energy and industry have failed to
preserve wife and children from famine and disease.

The total loss of a day's labour to the working man
is not only a social evil but a moral one. Disap-
pointment tends to make the industrious man dis-
contented with the institutions of the State and the
government of his country. Sometimes it carries
him from despair to vicious and criminal courses;
and when unable to supply his family with the
necessaries of life, he removes from so sad a spec-
tacle, and leaves his wife and offspring to the parish.

A scanty contribution by the community is an
inadequate substitute for the wages of labour, although it is a recognition of the workman's claim,
as "first creditor of the State,"* on property and
fixed incomes, the possessors of which are more
assured in their position than day-labourers.

Industry, therefore, ought to be encouraged, not
only on account of its high financial importance, but
also as it lays the foundation for, and mainly pre-

* E. Burke.

serves, the greatest patriotism and the highest social good. Toil, while in moderation, is neither injurious nor degrading. A poor-rate fails to bless entirely the giver or the receiver.

Gold does not perish or become burdensome to the State like unemployed labour. It has universal favour ; and if in the least degree interfered with by taxation or low rate of interest, it goes where interest is high or taxation light. It remains only where profitable investments are to be found, and where taxes are not oppressive.

If labour is dear, the employer must expect profits to be less, or his transactions to be limited and productive of anxiety and risk ; for the competition of lightly taxed foreign labour will supplant or depress his sales. Therefore he abandons his intention of employing labour at home, and transfers his capital, and a few only of his best workmen, to a less taxed country.

Hence, heavy taxes *deprive* native workmen of a source of profit. The labourer, mechanic, artisan, seaman, or miner, loses, not only from profit withheld, but from competition induced by financial causes. And when it is remembered that the loss of a single day's work can never be made up to the workman and his family, every one of common sense will admit the special care which his interests require, and the equity of giving a market and just profits to his labour, as far as the Legislature can do so.

The experience of all Financiers has proved that direct taxation upon capital has certain limits which cannot be transgressed without loss, and has verified the saying, that if you would raise millions, you must tax millions. Even the millions, however, cannot bear taxation, or afford a revenue to the State, if labour is very cheap and wages are very low. The right of franchise might be given to low-rented classes of our workmen, if their skill and fidelity are well known and recognised by engagements of trust in their parish. And it should be remembered, that the imperial and provincial taxes which a man pays, rather than his rent, should constitute his elective qualification.

For, in constitutional changes, it would be wise and beneficial to aim at men's social, as well as political, good. Thus, the privilege of voting should be made at once the reward of, and stimulant to, temperate and frugal habits, by annexing the qualification to moderate rents, combined with good conduct, rather than to high rents, combined with perhaps extravagant or intemperate habits. "The late ministry" (in their Reform Bill, so ably advocated by Sir Lytton Bulwer) "wisely departed from the old brick and mortar restrictions."*

How can a £10 house-rent of itself fit an individual for the just exercise of the elective franchise? How can idle or ignorant, dissipated citizens, so qualified, remain free men? or select diligent and

* Blackwood.

talented, instead of truthless and speculative candidates, who seek their suffrages that they may have votes to sell, or employ for their advancement in office, or in their profession, or to gratify vanity.

There are young mechanics and artisans, gardeners, ploughmen, bricklayers, smiths, herdsmen, foresters, quarriers, hedgers, masons, carpenters, drainers, miners, clerks, &c., who are the pride and honour of their country, from their good character and trustworthiness. Surely such men should not be debarred from the elective trust *and privilege* because rents are lower in villages than in great cities.

By wise and just arrangements labour might be represented. No respectable class who subsisted by hand labour should be excluded from this share of influence in the making of laws and imposing taxes, and the State would then rest on a pyramidal basis, instead of its present narrow pedestal.

It may be objected, that workmen demand more power, and would be satisfied with no elective right except manhood suffrage. I contend that they would. In the same spirit that you carry out the love of your neighbour, in the same measure will it be repaid, as the recent invitation to Sheriff Alison by Glasgow trades' unions testifies. This is not a mere assertion, but a conclusion founded on the declaration of the highest authority, and one which all human experience confirms.

Among those who seek to have political power

are many thoughtful and honourable minds who think their welfare at present utterly neglected, but who are sufficiently enlightened to be susceptible of rational arguments in support of gradual measures. They know that Greece and Rome were ruined by democracies, and discern between rash and reasonable modes of concession to their claims, and they feel that "a man's rights are not, as the world thinks, what is right others should do to him, but what is right he should do to others." *

They think, with the Comte de Cavour, one of the greatest statesmen in Europe, that "England's supremacy is a necessity for the world ; England represents the one great principle of abstract freedom; if it were possible that she could be worsted in a struggle with France, no free-born man would any longer be in safety on the entire continent of Europe."†

Under the present system, some men who have the right of franchise do not qualify, and many never vote. Men are contented when their class is qualified, and confide in the judgment of those whose circumstances and interests correspond with their own. They know that "government is the force of the general interests of society, bound together for her protection from the revolt or anarchy of those individual interests which continually seek to prevail

* Rev. C. Kingsley.
† Count Cavour on British Freedom.

against the community ; in other words, government is *the whole*—factions are *individual*. Like M. Thiers, we are for the *all* against the *some*, the existence of government is to our eyes one of the holiest forms, not only of good sense, but of public virtue. Administration is the mechanism of government. . . . . War, when just and necessary, is the collective heroism of nations—a supernatural self-devotion even to the death—elevating the warrior in his sense of right, in his enthusiasm for his native country far above the low interests of self-preservation—inflicting crimeless death, or fearlessly meeting it for the welfare of that civil community whose soldier he becomes."*

The occupier of the low-rented house in the village may possess far higher moral and mental qualifications for the elective franchise than the occupier of the £10 house in the metropolis ; and certainly might be much better fitted to select a properly qualified and worthy representative than the owners or occupiers of public-houses, gin-palaces, pawnbroking premises, gambling-houses, and lodging-houses for bad characters of both sexes.

Workmen who have the charge of property in mines, mills, quarries, woods, stores, cattle, granaries, manufactories, rail, canal, or road or sea-borne traffic ; toll-keepers, harbour-masters, road-surveyors, gar-

* Lamartine the Patriot.

deners, master carpenters, blacksmiths, although in places of great trust, live in villages or in small towns, and by Rural or Coast employments, and may occupy premises connected with their employments which pay less than £10 rent, if rented at all.

They, however, are employed in work which needs not only persevering toil, but skill in planning and execution ; and frequently such employments cannot be contracted for and executed by task work, but must be confided to their honest and faithful exertions and efforts requiring strength and ingenuity, and involving risk of health from atmospheric changes and accidents as severe as those to which soldiers and sailors are exposed.

It may be alleged that the votes conferred on men in virtue of their occupation of places of trust would be exercised in accordance with the views of the parties who had appointed to such places.

This consequence does not follow, because the same qualities which had procured the confidence of those from whom it was acquired would prevent the unworthy use of their franchise given by the State, and the sacrifice of their office would be preferred to that of their country.

Political opinions are so equally distributed, and fidelity so valuable and so prized, that if their honourable conduct failed to please one class of politicians, it would be admired and recompensed by those who were honoured by the support of such electors.

Places of trust and profit, and persons of REAL trustworthiness, would sometimes be transferred from the collision of opinion, but the truest qualification for political trust, *Integrity*, would be upheld, and the principle of representative institutions would be vindicated without any final loss to such patriotic voters, even in income.

Such workmen can and do pay parochial and most, if not all, provincial rates, creditably, support and educate their families, and are ready to assist the officers of justice in capturing incendiaries and thieves, and all criminals, with no other motive than a sense of duty. These men seek no reward for doing their duty but the testimony of their own conscience, and the conviction that they have vindicated the character of their country, and risked the vengeance of those who degrade it. The wealthy, who rise by the aid of such labourers to affluence, and have the aid of such labourers to keep their property safe from waste and from thieves, should neither forget the obligations they have incurred, nor should fail to acknowledge the merit and good offices of those who differ from themselves, solely by having been less fortunate, and by residing in a less costly locality.

The soldier, the sailor, the policeman, whose services and whose good character have been recognised in the pension granted by his sovereign, or by the certificate of his superior officer, or by his employer, should be rewarded by ranking amongst those intrusted with elective power, and be privileged to share the honours of the State.

The failure of the former amendments of the representation to remove the social evils of the working classes, awakens misgivings as to the sufficiency of the present test of qualification to protect labour.

Although the capital of the monied classes may have been augmented, the property of the working classes does not appear to have increased in value to an equal extent. Since the passing of the bill for amending the "representation of the people," police, hulks, prisons, penitentiaries, asylums, houses of refuge, and ragged schools, testify its insufficiency to reform the condition of the people, and intimate that there is still some part of the institutional edifice imperfect.

If it fails to shelter the workmen of the nation from want and crime, from vice and suffering ; if it has left unrepaired the character of the nation, and not reunited its members, the social part of the structure is incomplete. I may observe with truth and soberness, that a free government not only establishes a universal security against wrong, but that it also cherishes all the noblest powers of the human mind ; that it tends to banish both the mean and the ferocious vices.

Would the Government learn the origin of those evils which produce intemperance, vice, and crime, and necessitate expensive and painful remedial measures in poorhouses and prisons, it must do so by the enfranchisement of intelligent and experienced workmen of known worth and intelligence.

The prison and the policeman fail to restore such as have, by despair, been alienated from virtue and loyalty, and led to breaches of the laws by offences whose origin dates from the rejection of proffered labour or from involuntary idleness, and which are often the effects of wounded feelings and the sense of undeserved misery !

Many of the thoughtful and worthy of the industrious portions of the community think the sufferings of their class proceed from the want of adequate representation, and feel that members of the House of Commons might better know their wants, and be more able to instruct the Legislature as to their condition, prospects, and impressions. They sometimes see the commerce of the nation and the revenue fall away, together with the labourers' wages, and the burdens of the country augmented by the maintenance in the jail of those who heretofore contributed to the revenues of the State and of the parish. Morality suffers ; and for the kindness of the virtuous and benevolent are, alas ! substituted severity and indignation ! and the workmen become the weakness and disgrace of the community, when divested of their social reputation. For the virtues which guard the natural seminaries of the affections, are their only true and lasting friends. There is a "demand of well-informed men for the improvement of civil institutions, and that of all classes growing in intelligence, to be delivered from a degrading inferiority, and to be admitted to a share of political power, proportioned to their new importance."

If the Parliament knew the causes of poverty and of crime, from those whom the State has to coerce or to feed, from the parties who are made criminals and paupers, more care would be taken of their education and of their labour capital, as well as more sympathy felt for their condition.

" The workman is assailed by the head and tail of the Constitution."* The Parliament taxes the necessaries of life ; and, when workmen's living thereby requires higher wages, the manufacturer and the farmer have recourse to machinery. They say their capital does not yield its fair profit, if the labour capital becomes too heavy a charge on the articles taken to market.

It must be admitted that, under free trade, the foreign competitor, producing abroad food and clothing, might undersell them from cheapness of living in other countries ; and that, if they did not resort to machinery, they would be compelled to abandon business, because machinery would be exported.

Former elective rights in some burghs founded on a fire and a pot on it to cook food, have been thought

* B. Franklin.

objectionable, and taxable or rateable incomes have been substituted as a basis of elective rights, but limited by a rental qualification. Neither of these systems, however, professes to recognise labour as capital or property, and wages as income qualifying for the franchise, wherever located, unless occupying a £10 house.

Were the member of Parliament chosen by a greater number of freemen electors, combining good character with a rental which supported by direct and indirect taxes and parish rates, the safety, credit, and welfare of the nation, he would have a less number of complaining meetings, newspapers condemning his votes and opposing his re-election; and his support to the Government, whether Whig or Tory, would be less subject to suspicion or animadversion. Voters who elected him would not be so often taunted with reproaches for the unworthy use of their franchise in electing demagogues, who are appointed to defend the smuggling of opium by force into China from Hindus who are compelled to grow it; or to vote armaments, raised and maintained by taxes on British industry, to enrich a few Britons at the expense of India,—because so many would instruct him in the circumstances of the mass of the working classes, that he could neither misrepresent nor fail to give a true view of the wants and sorrows of the working classes.

Strikes of workmen from reduction of wages, or from undue length of working hours in factories, or unfair weights or measures for miners' work, would be rarely, if ever, brought before Parliament, and made sources of irritation and discontent between masters and men, and of suffering to industrious families.

Were labour considered capital, and character a qualification for elective rights, every Christian congregation might be empowered to nominate individuals in proportion to their number, one or more, from their body, to vote for a member of the House of Commons.

Men who devote their income to educate children of both sexes—to obey parents, to act honestly, to speak truthfully, to do no violence, to honour the sovereign, and to love their neighbours—ought to be represented not only for their worth, but as public benefactors. "The laws which regulate religious thought must be the same with those which regulate our thoughts on all other subjects." * All who insure their lives for their families and themselves deserve the franchise. Property in friendly societies should be represented on the same wise reasoning which has suggested savings' bank property for qualification.

" In truth, there is the greatest difference between man and man ; and, instead of it being an easy thing to find a man qualified for a trust, there is nothing more difficult. Everybody knows this in practice.

* Rev. Mr. Maurice.

Everybody knows that if an employment requires intelligence, honesty, fidelity, disinterestedness, vigilance, knowledge of character, and a power of seeing through appearances as well as meeting surprises, he may search far and wide and not find the man. Yet these are the qualities that make a good elector, and without them a voter, be he rich or poor, is but 'leather and prunella.' " *

Representatives elected by such characters would be well fitted to economize the expenditure of the State and to counteract the undue influence of £10 rental qualifications derived from premises raised in value by the intemperate and dishonest and dissolute, who ultimately become inmates of penitentiaries and prisons, and require poor and police rates to support them in costly and unprofitable idleness.

Every one who had saved the life of a fellow-creature, who had devoted life to the care of cholera and typhus patients, or, as a constable or parish or town officer, obtained testimony to the faithful discharge of public duties, might well be trusted with the right of choosing members. Men who act for the benefit and safety of the nation and the sovereign, who have been intrusted with the care of factories, warehouses, granaries, railways, canals, and charges public and private ; and men who volunteer and arm in defence of their country, or who man life-boats ; and Under-Guardians or Man-

* *Times*

agers of Asylums for the Blind, Deaf and Dumb, Lunatic Asylums, Hospitals, Infirmaries, Poorhouses ; Head-clerks of Companies ; Mates and Masters of Vessels ; Station Masters ; Warehousemen ; Foremen ; and all in similar situations of trust,—would make a safe, powerful, and excellent constituency.

Rental, in so far only as it is the test of taxation, imperial, provincial, and local, is a suitable foundation for representative claims. Neither are the revenues of the State dependent so much on high rental of individuals as upon the number of occupants who consume commodities on which the Excise and Customs duties are collected.

A £10 house is, in great cities, often the receptacle of lodgers, who hire apartments from the occupier of premises, of which he is merely rent collector and house porter, and supplies voters inferior to a £5 rental in Wales, in Cornwall, or in Scotland.

Whether this £10 be gathered from the profits of thieving and fraudulent transactions, or from the more disgusting contributions of sensuality and intemperance, it should not only cease to *qualify*, but it should, in every such case, *dis*qualify such householders from voting.

As a corrective to the existing system, not only the respectable £10 tenants, but the parties contributing to a £10 rent of a widow, as lodgers, might, if of unquestionably good character, be also partakers of the elective privilege to the extent of one vote, provided the lodgers contributed, in the aggregate, as much to the National Exchequer by a direct tax, as the householder contributed to the local burdens : for each of them has £130 or £140 of the parents' capital practically embodied in his rearing and education—in truth, good principles and a trade, instead of savings' bank investments, which may not be so conducive to his habits of exertion, and to the value of his services to the community.

The object of the preceding pages has been to attract a greater degree of attention to the value of character and industrial exertions in constituting subjects of enfranchisement, whether in great or small cities—in town or in the country.

Rental, how much soever it may be suggested as a test of vote-worthiness, by a prudent consideration for the safety of wealth and for the promotion of frugality, is as inferior to known trustworthiness and industry for a basis of Parliamentary representation, as a machine is to a man.

Mr. Ricardo, in proposing to pay off part of the Debt, and Mr. M'Ewan, and those patriotic and just men who are willing to be subjected to a higher rate of taxation in proportion to the higher amount of their income, deserve the real gratitude of every one of their countrymen, and will, I trust, yet be listened to with respect, and have their views adopted by the most wealthy of the community.

If trustworthy and trusted voters should be considered dependent on their employers, there might be afforded by them the best class *for the ' Ballot' expedient.*

They would not injure those who confided private or public interests to their care, their own welfare being identified with the prosperity of their employers and of their country.

Bur since, alas! ignoble age must come,
Disease, and death's irrevocable doom,
The life which others yield let us bestow,
And give to fame what we to nature owe;
Great if we fall, and honoured if we live;
Or let us glory gain or glory give.—Iliad.

Νῦν δ'—ἔμπης γὰρ Κῆρες ἐφεστᾶσιν θανάτοιο
Μυρίαι, ἃς οὐκ ἔστι φυγεῖν βροτὸν οὐδ' ὑπαλύξαι—
Ἴομεν, ἠέ τῳ εὖχος ὀρέξομεν, ἠέ τις ἡμῖν.

HOMERI ILIADOS, Lib. xii. 310-328.

APPENDIX.

Extract from Letter, MR. JAMES LORIMER *to* LORD JOHN RUSSELL.

BY giving their due influence to wealth, to learning, and to other forms of social importance and individual worth, alongside of a wide, if not a universal, recognition of mere citizenship, it seems to me that a measure might be prepared which would go far to supersede the necessity of farther constitutional changes; and it would be in the highest degree gratifying to Englishmen that such a measure should proceed from one to whom they are already indebted for so many services.

APPENDIX.

THE true principle of society is, that every one should serve. The result, if this were carried out fully, would be that every one (being served by every other one) would rule, yet rather by the desire of others than his own.

Ignorant, selfish people cannot be free, among whom the spirit prevails of each caring for his own welfare, and of being careless and unconcerned for that of his neighbour, whether rich or poor, or those who are indifferent to the public prosperity. Such people cannot be free. The aim and object of every true Christian patriot is to help forward a reform of the people themselves, that they may learn the truth, and the "truth shall make them free, whether the chief of the government be king or senate," * &c.

Since the foregoing went to press, I have been much gratified to find myself anticipated in the principal object aimed at in these pages by my friend Mr. George John Cayley, of Wydale, Yorkshire. The following are some short extracts from

* Mr. Hamilton of St. Eruans, on Truth and Error.

his lively and really admirable pamphlet, entitled—
" The Working Classes ; their interest in Adminis-
trative, Financial, and Electoral Reform ;" to the
whole of which I venture to refer my readers :—

Those who know the working classes of England well,
know that they are worthy to be trusted. Those who
would not trust them have formed a false opinion of them
from an insignificant minority, composed of the noisiest and
worst of their class. It is want of knowledge of one another
which makes classes distrust each other. We are all children of our Divine Father ; we are all made by the same
Omniscient Creator, in the same eternal image. The
hearts of all classes beat with the same human impulses ;
our veins all run with blood of the same colour. But if
some of the upper classes are over-suspicious of the lower,
the same unnecessary mistrust exists in the minds of too
many of the working classes towards those who are placed
above them by the accidents of birth and fortune.

*   *   *   *

The law should strike keenly and sternly at those political footpads who waylay honest voters in the street ; those
door-to-door burglars of the poor man's freedom. Let public life be absolutely public ; public speaking, public
influence, public voting. Let there be no whispering be-
hind doors ; no winks that mean bribery ; no nods that
mean intimidation. Still less let us give up public freedom
and public spirit as a bad job. Still less let us have
wavering, guilty hands trembling on the wrong side of
dark boxes, which would be the coffins of the dignity of an
Englishman's franchise. Let us learn self-respect enough
to do our duty to our country in the face of day.

*   *   *   *

MONEY REFORM has more vital bearing on the destinies of the working classes, than many of the clap-trap cries and nostrums of popular agitation. The working man's interest in sound finance and good government is all the deeper because he is the first to suffer by bad finance measures and bad government.

*   *   *   *

The power of the working classes, and their influence on public measures, consist directly in the SUFFRAGE, and indirectly in the force of PUBLIC OPINION.

We want something more than a mere brick-and-mortar test of political wisdom and independence. It is the man who lives in the house, not the house which shelters the man, we want to inquire about.

We should admit to the franchise all such men as by their intelligence, trustworthiness, and social position, seem likely to be worthy of the franchise. How can we classify and define such voters? First,—Every man who can show by the entries in his labour book (kept for this purpose, and in which it should be felony to forge an entry) that he has earned £50 by his labour in the year previous to registration, and that he has resided in the borough for which he aspires to vote, during the year previous to such registration. Secondly,—Every man employed at a salary of £80 and upwards, resident in the borough during the year previous to registration. Thirdly,—Every man trusted in his vocation with the reception of uncounted money (as, for instance, clerks at railway booking counters, cashiers of tradesmen, and the like) down to those receiving salaries of £30 a year. Fourthly,—Every daily schoolmaster or teacher intrusted on the average of the year previous to registration with the education of at least a dozen boys. All these, and similar classes of men, whose trust-worthiness and intelligence are witnessed and approved by the practical confidence placed in them by their fellow-men, should have a voice in the affairs of the nation, whether they rent a four-storey house, or a garret at eighteenpence a week.

Depend upon it the men who are climbing on the national tree, and who hope some day to get somewhere near the top, or at least to be able to give their children a lift above the lower branches—the men who are climbing, and who know how to climb, are not likely to lay their axes to the constitutional roots, in order to have a scramble for acorns when it falls. They may cry out to have rotten boughs lopped away here and there. They may cry out to have the bitter gall-nuts of official jobbery picked off the branches they are cankering. But still they love the good old tree.

***

RIGHTS OF LABOUR.

" Would the song of the shirt ever have been sung had the needlewomen been united for self-protection ?" Theirs is labour at the mercy of capital, and to what capitalists have brought it let our graveyards bear witness.

It is easy for Dives to sit in his parlour and preach the extreme doctrine of supply and demand, but it is hard for Lazarus to understand it. Indeed, by the same kind of extreme reasoning, free-trade could be shown to mean free-booting; for the cheapest market is where the power is strong enough to make its own terms for articles required. But why are the societies of working men to be written and spoken of as an evil, while a firm adherence to party is looked upon as the protecting principle of the middle and upper classes ? Why are the stands made by working men against the inroads of power to be written and spoken down, while the classes above them are glorified for similar conduct ? How long are the words *right* and *wrong* to have two distinct meanings—one for the rich and another for the poor man ?

From the press, the platform, and even the pulpit, nothing is more common than to have the advantages of combined energy and concentrated effort recommended and enforced with great eloquence ; indeed, society in general is but a gigantic combination of the whole to protect the individual members of which it is composed. It is therefore strange that one occupying the respectable position of member for the city should be so foolish as to counsel his fellow-citizens, and working men generally, not to act upon the principle of union amongst themselves, which every day's experience shows to be so beneficial. Small as is the intelligence of the working classes, I need scarcely say that they despise and laugh at such miserable twaddle as this. They cannot shut their eyes to the fact that the merchant, the lawyer, and even the ministers of the crown, do all that they can to rise to a higher sphere—in short, to gain a better position in the world ; and why should the working man not strive to improve his condition also ?

" We hear in these days a great deal respecting rights ; the rights of private judgment, the rights of labour, the rights of property, and the rights of man. Rights are grand things, divine things in this world of God's; but the way in which we expound these rights is the very incorporation of selfishness.

c

" Let the people be educated; let there be a fair field and no favour; let every man have a fair chance, and then the happiest condition of a nation would be, that when every man had been educated morally and intellectually to his very highest capacity, there should then be selected out of men so trained a Government of the wisest and the best."[*]

Mr. Spackman, on Occupations of the People, pages 6 and 7, says :—

" Machinery, as applied to the cultivation of the soil, is yet in its infancy. . . . If this mighty power of production could be carried on *ad infinitum*, it would present the extraordinary anomaly of the accumulation of great wealth with the condition of the labouring classes in a course of gradual deterioration. . . . The increase in the production of manufactured goods and the employment of the population proceed in an inverse ratio to each other."

The *Times* of Saturday, May 4, 1850, says :—

" Mr. Slaney's motion, on Tuesday night, as explained by his speech, and recommended by a life of philanthropical exertion, deserves all but our highest respect and unqualified sympathy; his cause is sacred, his facts are grave, his philosophy not quite superficial ; and, altogether, he is such a man as we would wish to keep in the House as a witness to the evils of our social condition. We cannot deny a word that he says. We do not wish to deny it. We even thank him for obtruding on this busy world facts of such painful and serious import. But it must be confessed that his statements excite a distress which his counsels are not equal to remove."

* Rev. F. Robertson.

The *Times* asks, Does it not appear at first sight a strange result of the terrible statistics of society that, upon an average, one person out of twenty of the inhabitants of this luxurious metropolis is every day destitute of food and employment, and every night without a place for shelter or repose ?

In conclusion, we must remind the reader that society is a pyramid, in which each social grade increases in extent, the lower we go. It is the fashion with some to declaim against the vices and luxury of the wealthier classes. If they would see these removed, they must apply a lever to the whole bulk of society. They must begin by raising and improving the poor and poorest classes ; and, when this is done, they will soon discover that the upper orders are hastening to improve themselves. Moral and intellectual worth will supersede rank and wealth, as the criterion of " position " and the key to power.

Another *enormous* source of evil is the way in which the poorer classes of our city are crowded together, to the utter disregard of everything like decency. This contributes fearfully to the profligacy of the lower orders,—and no measures of social improvement are more needful than those which aim at a remedy. To use the words of the pastor of a large parish in Glasgow :—" The physical circumstances of the poor paralyse all the efforts for their spiritual or moral welfare. . . . . Every effort to create a spiritual tone of feeling is counteracted by a set of physical circumstances which is incompatible with the exercise of common morality. Talk of morality amongst people who herd—men, women, and children together, with no regard to age or sex—in one narrow confined apartment ! You might as well talk of cleanliness in a sty, or of limpid purity in the contents of a cesspool." *

SCOTTISH HOME MISSIONS.

From the *North British Review, February* 1859.

"In fact, in those vast wildernesses of streets, and lanes, and noisome courts and alleys, of which the lower parts of our great cities consist, while the worst vices of social life are generated to the utmost, society, in the true sense of the word, can be scarcely said to exist.

"Affection, trust, mutual help, generosity, self-sacrifice, public spirit, and whatever else is most noble in human action and human suffering, droop and wither as in an element unfriendly to their life.

"Meanwhile, with so few supports and aids to virtue, seductions and incentives to evil abound on every side. While the restraints on vicious indulgence are few, the means of such indulgence are perilously accessible and near. The god of this world spreads here his richest banquet, and provides his seductive but poisoned viands for every variety of taste. The dram-shop glares at every step ; the low farce, and the vile casino, and those other haunts and dens of sin, allure the passer-by at every turn.

"In an age of large towns, and specially in the largest cities, the Church most feebly and inadequately maintains the conflict. *There* where the expansive powers of the nations and of the Church may be best tested and compared, the nation outgrows the Church.

"Thus, while in 1811 the population was increasing at the rate of 14·3 per cent. in ten years, church accommoda-

* Rev. Dr. Norman Macleod, Barony, Glasgow.

tion only increased at the rate of 6·8 per cent. ; and in 1851, population was increasing at the rate of 12·6 per cent., and church accommodation increased at the rate of 9·4.

" In Glasgow the word ' Wynds' was immediately suggestive of ideas of filth and debasement, both physical and moral. Now a Christian Church has been set up in the most confined and crowded locality, as if to rebuke for ever, and to render inexcusable, all unbelief as to the efficacy of the Gospel to elevate the character and to ameliorate the condition even of the most sunken of our population.

" As might have been expected, the pressure of the times has been severely felt by the congregation. Not a few members are at present suffering great privations, and some fifteen or twenty of them are unable to attend church, in consequence of having been compelled to part with their clothing for the purpose of obtaining food, and paying rent and taxes. In spite of these unfavourable circumstances, the sum raised by the Congregation is highly creditable to them. With some assistance from a few friends, they have contributed for all purposes, during the last fifteen months, the sum of £200, 8s. 5¼d.,—of that sum £89 was raised by collections at the church-door.

CURIOUS RELIGIOUS STATISTICS.

From the evidence (just published) taken before the Lords' Select Committee on Church-rates, which sat towards the close of last session, we have culled some facts bearing on the relative position both of the Church of England and of the leading Nonconformist sects towards the population at large. According to calculations based upon accurate *data*, and carefully made, there are 7,546,948 actual church-going men of the Church of England, or 42 per cent. of the gross population ; and 4,466,266 nominal Churchmen, but practically of no church, or 25 per cent. of the gross population. So that the field of operation of her clergy, ministerial and missionary, is spread over 67 per cent., or 12,013,214 of the community at large. On the other hand, the chapel-going Roman Catholics in England amount to 610,786, or 3½ per cent. of the whole population ; the chapel-going Baptists (six different kinds) to 457,181, or 2¼ per cent. ; the chapel-going Independents are 1,297,861, or 7¼ per cent. ; the chapel-going Wesleyan Methodists (seven different kinds) are 2,264,321, or 13 per cent. ; and all other " Protestant" Dissenters, including in the number Jews and Mormons, are estimated at 1,286,246, or 6¾ per cent. The total of worshipping or *bonâ fide* Protestant Dissenters is 5,303,609, or 29½ per cent. of the gross population. Again, there is an alarming picture presented of the irreligion in which large masses of the population are steeped. For example, in Southwark there are 68 per cent. of the people who attend no place of worship ; in Lambeth, 60½ ; in Sheffield, 62 ; in Oldham, 61½ ; in Gateshead, 60 ; in Preston, 59 ; in Brighton, 54 ; in the Tower Hamlets, 53½ ; in Finsburgh, 53 ; in Salford, 52 ; in South Shields, 52 ; in Manchester, 51½ ; in Bolton, 51½ ; in Stoke, 51½ ; in Westminster, 50 ; and in Coventry, 50. So that in all those places, except the two last-named cities, the odds are on the side of those who habitually absent themselves from every religious service whatever. Of 34 of the great towns of England, embracing an aggregate population of 3,993,467, 2,197,388, or 52½ per cent. of the community are wholly non-worshipping. But this is, beyond question, to some extent attributable to the want of church accommodation, for the evidence goes to show that the sitting accommodation provided by the Church of England and Nonconformists together is only 57 per cent. of the whole population, and of this 27 per cent. is furnished by the Dissenters,—12 per cent. by the Wesleyans, who alone during the last 12 months have spent about £100,000 in chapel - building. The sum expended annually in the repairs of the fabrics and the maintenance of the church services is nearly £500,000, of which only about £250,000 is raised by rate. There having been no ecclesiastical census before 1851, few or no reliable means exist for comparing the religious phenomena of the present day with those of half a century or a century ago ; but, in answer to the Archbishop of Canterbury, the Rev. Dr. Hume, the incumbent of a parish, populous and poor, in Liverpool, and a witness before the committee, expressed his conviction, founded on long experience and observation, that the large masses of the population who attend no place of worship whatever are in danger of being lost not only to the Church, but to religion altogether. The population of the country, always on the increase, is becoming more and more a town population. In 1851 there were 9,000,000 living in towns of 10,000 people and upwards, and only 8,000,000 in smaller towns, in villages, and in rural districts. Dr. Hume apprehends that at the close of the present century 70 per cent. of the gross population will be located in large towns ; and, therefore, he adds, if our large towns are left to themselves, practical heathenism must inevitably outgrow Christianity.

I ask my readers how many public-houses they know that could exist for a single year unless they were supported by wickedness ? How many that could thrive if supported only by the weary traveller, the temperate festive party, or the industrous tradesman or farmer ? How many where the sober will not be permitted to get tipsy, and the tipsy drunk ? How many who will refuse whisky to that miserable wretch who is robbing wife and children to pamper his vile passions ?—or to that mother and wife who, lost to all sense of shame, has become a notorious drunkard ?

I believe the working people are generally much in favour of the Mackenzie Act, and especially the female portion. The men like it well also, because before, when they got into a house with a party, they didn't like to break up the party, but now the Act does it for them, and they are able to go to their work in the morning. I have heard some of the men who were given to intemperance say, that they considered the Act as a great boon, because it removed temptations. In this they referred particularly to the mornings. It used to be a common habit to drink in the morning, and the Act removed the facilities for this habit being indulged in.

What we wish to make plain is, that the working classes are fast entitling themselves to a voice in the representation by the only way in which they at present can, viz., by their wealth. This a return relative to savings' banks recently laid before Parliament enables us approximately to do. From this return we learn that on the 20th of November last the amount of deposits in savings' banks was no less than £33,921,881, contributed by 1,383,202 depositors. On an average, therefore, each depositor had invested very nearly £25. And if in any new Reform Bill that may be passed there should be a clause enfranchising all who had £40 in the savings' bank, assuming each to have deposited that sum, the aggregate deposits would add 843,000 to the electoral roll—about four-fifths as many as the whole number of persons.

The following table shows the number and character of the depositors, with the amounts deposited :—·

			Number of Depositors.	Amount of Deposits including Interest.
Not exceeding	£1	.	200,485	£60,628
Do.	5	.	276,345	701,377
Do.	10	.	181,852	1,271,999
Do.	15	.	131,480	1,575,708
Do.	20	.	80,825	1,385,197
Do.	30	.	139,654	3,356,587
Do.	40	.	113,205	3,764,214
Do.	50	.	54,149	2,402,454
Do.	75	.	89,267	5,418,339
Do.	100	.	42,602	3,693,429
Do.	125	.	28,481	3,157,947
Do.	150	.	16,800	2,294,713
Do.	200	.	26,560	4,511,645
Exceeding	200	.	1,494	327,644
			1,383,202	£33,921,881

Some of the depositors may not strictly belong to the operative class, but there can be no doubt whatever that the majority of them do.

But this sum in the savings' banks, large as it is, does not represent the entire substantiality of the working classes. In the hands of friendly, mutual benefit, and other similar societies which the forethought of workmen has established with the view of keeping the wolf from the door in times of sickness, and death, and old age, there are very large sums, how much, we have no means of ascertaining, but we observe from the return under our notice that £1,562,784 have been deposited in savings' banks by 9994 friendly societies. From other sources of information we are aware that there are about 27,000 registered friendly societies in Great Britain, besides an almost incalculable number which have not taken advantage of the Registration Act. The amount of money possessed by such associations will therefore, in all probability, amount to £10,000,000 or £15,000,000. This, added to the sum in the savings' banks, would give from £40,000,000 to £50,000,000 in all to be placed to the credit of the working classes of this country—a sum representing an average saving of about 30s. for each man, woman, and child in the United Kingdom. It is clear, therefore, to our thinking, that, on the ground of property alone, the working classes may very justly claim a larger measure of representation than that which they now enjoy. A class possessing £50,000,000 is not one that should be politically ignored—especially when, as in this case, it represents so much industry, carefulness, and intelligent forethought. And it cannot long be ignored.

LABOUR CAPITAL IN THE COUNTRY.

Probable cost of a young man to his parents until 15 years of age :—

BOARD AND LODGING.

1 to 5 years, 1s. 6d. per week,	.	£19 10 0		
5 to 10 „ 2s. „	.	26 0 0		
10 to 15 „ 3s. „	.	39 0 0		
			£84 10 0	

CLOTHES.

1 to 5 years, £1 per annum, .	£5 0 0		
5 to 10 „ £1, 10s. „ .	7 10 0		
10 to 15 „ £2 „ .	10 0 0		
		22 10 0	

SCHOOL AND BOOKS.

5 to 10 years, 1s. per month,	.	£3 5 0	
10 to 15 „ 2s. „	.	6 10 0	
		9 15 0	
		£116 15 0	

Young men after 15 years of age, if in health, are considered able to provide for themselves,—add three more years to a young man, and his cost will be £137, 9s., which appears a very just estimate of the cost of a working man's children.

REDHILL SEMINARY FOR YOUTH—NEAR LONDON.

For clothing, food, and washing, police charges, &c., ...	£15 11 9
Superintendence, teaching, training, furniture, taxes, &c., ...	14 3 0
Extras, as office and advertising, . .	1 6 0
	£31 0 9

But Redhill expenses may come to be diminished to the following sum :—

For food, clothing, and washing,	.	£13
Superintendence, teaching, &c.,	.	10
Extras, ...	.	2 to £4

or about £25 per annum. Then, when we remember that the labour of each would be more productive as the difficulties of the soil were overcome, and that at Mettray each boy's labour now produces £8 per annum, we may safely alter this figure to £20 per boy per annum, or about £4000 a year, as the expense of maintaining each establishment, or ONE MILLION STERLING for the two hundred and fifty.

The cost of bringing a young man at prime of life, or eighteen years old, valued at £150, at 7 per cent., is £10, 10s. He has cost to his parents, or has, with aid from his small acquisitions, been reared to the rural employments, Drainer, Shoemaker, Wright, Tailor, Woodman, Ploughman, Shepherd, Cattle Herd, Miner, Quarrier, Roadman, Hedger, Dyke-builder, Mason, Turner, Weaver, Printer, Plasterer, Gardener, Canal or Railway Stoker, Engineman, or Horse Driver.

I am in receipt of your favour of 22d inst., and but for having been from home would have been answered sooner.

In reply to your first question, I may say that the average rental paid by young married men in town of the respectable portion of the working classes is, for one room and kitchen, £8 to £9, and two rooms and kitchen, £10 to £11, per annum ; and second, the expense of lodgings for the working classes runs about 4s. per week, for two persons in one room, making 2s. each. The better classes frequently pay 5s. per week for two in one room respectably furnished, and clerks and warehousemen may even go the length of 6s. for a room in a superior locality. From my own experience, I know that these are the average prices paid.

Working Class Suffrage.

To the Editor of the Courant.

Sir,—In discussing the question of reform, it is held out, on the one hand, that if the qualification of voters is reduced so low as contended for by Mr. Bright and others, it would introduce as voters a number greater than the whole classes of voters at present on the rolls, and in this way would swamp and outnumber the whole of the upper and middle classes, and throw the whole power of Parliament into the hands of one class. On the other hand, it is alleged, on the part of the working classes, that if the bulk of them have no vote they are not represented, and have no voice in the imposing of taxes, of which they must pay their share.

In considering how far these objections can be remedied, with a due adherence to the principle of every class being represented as nearly as possible in proportion to their intelligence and property, the following plan of arrangement has occurred, and is suggested for consideration, viz., That, leaving the qualification for the burghs and counties to remain as at present to the classes possessing these qualifications, there should be a new class introduced—say all that are rated and actually pay poor rates, or who have been householders for six months; but that this extended class should not all be entitled to be voters for the member, but that they should choose from their own body a list of those they consider to be most intelligent and respectable as delegates, to meet, act, and vote with the other voters on the roll. Such list to be equal to about one-fifth or one-sixth of the voters of the other class previously on the roll.

If this plan was adopted, then the meeting of this new class of voters would require to be held on the day preceding the day of voting for the member, and to this meeting there would fall to be furnished a certified list of the number of the other classes of voters on the roll at the time for the district, so that the meeting might be able to fix the number of the delegates to be chosen by them as voters—say equal to one-fifth or one-sixth of the number on the certified roll of the district, as being supposed to be about the fair amount in proportion to the property of those holding the new qualification. In referring to this proportion, it may be observed that a considerable number of the voters on the previous rolls, will, at each election, from illness, distance, or other causes, not be present to vote for the member, while the delegates chosen by the new set of voters will all be sure to attend ; and in this way the new voters, although nominally only one-fifth or one-sixth, would practically be in general equal to at least one-fourth of those attending and voting at each election.

In this way, while the whole working classes would be represented, and have delegates to express their views and wishes ; they could not, on the other hand, be brought into the list of voters in such numbers as to swamp or over-power the other classes. According to this rule each class would have a fair proportion of votes and consideration in choosing the member, and the means of bringing under his notice and observation their different views, objects, and interests. ALPHA. W. P.,

A very respected and aged Whig.

EXTRACT FROM SPEECH OF MR. BRIGHT AT LIVERPOOL.

At this hour 24,000,000 of people in this country lived
in houses of less rental than £10 per annum, and only
6,000,000 lived in houses of a higher rental than £10.
The conclusion, then, to be drawn from all these facts is,
that the revenue produced by taxation upon the ordinary
articles of consumption falls heaviest upon the industrious
classes. He (Mr. Bright) lived in the midst of a manufacturing district, and he knew something of the life of the
labouring man. Although this was a time of unusual prosperity, the life of labouring men was one of peculiar hard-
ship and difficulty. Labouring men have to maintain an
incessant struggle to keep themselves from what they dread
so much—the workhouse. Their life is precarious, and, on
the average, not of long duration.

ADDRESS OF THE CENTRAL ASSOCIATION OF MASTER
BUILDERS TO THEIR WORKMEN.

Friends and Fellow-Citizens,—Next session Parliament
will be required practically to confide to your order, as a
majority of the contemplated constituency, the trust and
power of making laws for the government not only of
yourselves but of the rest of the community. Would it
not be prudent to remember that the determination of the
Legislature will be guided by the opinion they will form
of your fitness to execute the trust, and of the safety to
their own rights and interests of placing such powers in
your hands? The eyes of the whole country are anxiously
directed to your conduct. Nothing is more timid than
capital, nothing more sensitive than established authority.

Alarm the enfranchised classes by unreasonable demands or popular excesses, and to what decision will they come ? If the legislation of trades' unions is to be transferred from the council-room of the conference to the House of Commons, where will be our liberties ? Your interests and ours are reciprocal. Out of the same fund, by the same works, we get our common living. " Of the head and the hands neither can say to the other, ' I have no need of thee.'" We heartily acknowledge our obligations to your skill and industry. To our capital you are indebted for their profitable application. With sincere respect for your many valuable qualities, we would, dismissing all heat and temper from our councils, invite you, in a perfectly friendly, but also in a very plain and downright way, to consider the unnatural spirit of opposition which at present estranges us from one another.[*]

---

[*] So far from strikes being approved, they are discouraged as much as possible. I quote the following from one of the most influential of the societies, the *Carpenters' and Joiners' Circular :—*

" The experience of the past has taught us not to expend our means in a futile attempt, by strikes, to enhance the price of, and command a market for, our labour, but by profitably employing our surplus hands, convert their toil into a means of wealth for all, and save them from the consciousness of trenching on the incomes and comforts of their fellow-workmen."

I also maintain that the object of these societies is in itself beneficial, as stated in the opening clause of the same rules, being "to establish an institution which shall afford facilities to the members in meeting together for the transaction of business, the study of science, and for mutual improvement, apart from the pernicious influence of the public-house."

The method of proposing, seconding, and balloting for members is the same as at a club, and equally tends to exclude objectionable persons. These rules do not compel uniformity of wages, though they fix the minimum at 5s. 6d. a day. Regulations regarding skilled workmen and taskwork are the same in effect as in the Government contracts, and in deciding the minimum price of labour, they only do the same as the ironmasters, who regulate

NOTE ON FINANCE.

From *Tracts on Protection*, No. I.

" The increasing riches of the kingdom seem only to diminish, instead of enlarging the command which the sons of toil have of the necessaries of life. This opposition of interests is not accounted for by the inevitable disparity in the conditions of men—a thing to be wondered at, but endured : a law of man's inexplicable fate. It is evidently connected with a deficient regulation, or an ill regulation, of the relations of men to each other. It is a disease very plainly proceeding from something improperly ordered in the political system. It is an evident perversion of the wholesome organization of society to purposes contrary to that universal justice which is the end and object of all society."

---

the minimum price of iron. Doubtless, the Ironmasters' Society or Union has its "blacks" (those who undersell the quarterly fixed prices), the same as the bricklayers stigmatize as their "blacks" those who work when others are on strike.

The rules for the maintenance of order and sobriety are excellent, and there is no doubt that the quiet behaviour of the men on all occasions (particularly when they were locked out on Saturday) is mainly attributable to such regulations.

Since the establishment of these societies, the conduct of the metropolitan building workmen has immensely improved; the workhouse is comparatively unknown to them, and dishonesty is equally rare.

The rules of the Masons' Society are a perfect study ; they partake very much of the admirable German system for travelling artisans. They have upwards of 200 lodges throughout the country, and any one transgressing against "sobriety, decency, or morality," is reported and punished by the society. According to their statement, they "wish to place themselves in such a position as shall gain the esteem of all good men."

STRIKES.

In strikes you combine to do a thing which is impossible, and in the attempt to do which you are yourselves subjected to the severest privations. Therefore, what I recommend is, not to combine against your master, who is the victim merely of the currency laws, but to combine against the laws which create these great changes in the currency—and you will carry with you the whole of society. There is no man of any sense in the country who won't join with you in the effort to make such a change in the currency laws as will prevent these fatal changes in prices, and with them wages and profits. I will conclude by making one observation, and it is this: I will give you an idea of the enormous extent of the loss inflicted on the country by these monetary crises to which I have alluded. There have been four great monetary crises in our own recollections—those of 1825, 1838, 1847, and 1857. Not one of these crises has occurred without causing a loss of no less than 100 millions on the country—the last much more; the bankruptcies in 1857 alone were £45,000,000. The monetary crises which have occurred since the passing of the bill of 1819 have inflicted upon the community a loss of not less than 500 millions sterling. To do away with the probability of such loss occurring again, is an object worth striving for. The present system is, that holders of money issue money to all persons engaged in speculations, however absurd, and, when the money comes to be paid, up goes the discount. There is ruin spread over the country, to an extent which would be inconceivable to those who have not witnessed it.—SIR A. ALISON, Bart.

www.ingramcontent.com/pod-product-compliance
Lightning Source LLC
Chambersburg PA
CBHW030905260626
47169CB00008B/2702